THE YOUNG·MERLIN·TRILOGY
BOOK ONE

PASSAGER

JANE YOLEN

D0181196

SCHOLASTIC INC.

New York Toronto London Auckland Sydney

To Michael Stearns,
passager indeed

Acknowledgment

This book is based on the short story "The Wild Child" from the collection
Merlin's Booke, but has been significantly expanded and refocused.

ISBN 0-590-37073-1

12 11 10 9 8 7 6 5 4 3 2 1   8 9/9 0 1 2 3/0

Printed in the U.S.A.   40

First Scholastic printing, September 1998

Text set in Fairfield Medium
Designed by Kaelin Chappell

CONTENTS

Passager:

A falcon caught in the wild
and trained by the falconer,
but not yet a mature bird.

Dark.

Night.

"He is still asleep, Mother."

"Three drops of the tincture will keep him still."

"Must we leave him?"

"We must."

"But he is so young."

"He is old enough. And we cannot keep him with us longer. There is danger to us all if he stays."

"But there is danger for him here."

"That is why we are leaving him high in the tree. The wild dogs cannot climb, nor fox nor wolves. In the daytime he will be quick and bright. He knows his nuts and berries, his mushrooms and ferns. You

have taught him well. He will be found soon enough by the wild men of the woods, the wodewose, those without a place, whose villages have been erased by plague. They will hold him close as we cannot."

"But he is such a little bird, my child, my owlet, my hawkling."

"If you keep him longer, he will be your death. And ours. The church forbids it. God's law. And man's."

"I would die for him, Mother."

"Let him live for you. Come. Morning will be here soon enough and it is already time for Matins. We dare not miss more than that or there will be talk."

Light.

Day.

1. TERRITORY

THE BOY WAS SNIFFING AT THE ROOT OF A TREE, trying to decide if it was worth eating the mushrooms there, when he heard the first long baying of the pack. It was a sound that made the little hairs on the back of his neck stand up.

He turned at the sound and tried to find its source, but this was a dark part of the woods, and tangled. He was still considering when the first dog broke through the underbrush, almost at his heels.

It was a dun-colored dog, long-snouted, long-bodied. He had enough time to see that. He struck at it with the stick he always carried and it scrabbled away from him, whining.

He did not wait for the rest of the pack to find him, but jumped for the lower branch of the tree and scrambled up.

Finding its courage, the dun dog leaped for him and its teeth grazed his ankle, but it missed its hold.

The boy climbed higher, fear lending him quickness, strength. He was already high up in the tree when the rest of the pack found him. They broke through the brambles and bayed at the foot of the tree. There were seven of them, one more than the last time. The boy counted them off on his fingers—one hand's worth and a thumb had been the number the last time. There was a new one, a large yellow mastiff. He did not like the look of the dog. It was big and had brutal jaws. Clearly it had taken over leadership of the pack from the dun.

There was nothing the boy could do but wait them out. He had done it before. Patience was his one virtue, his necessity. Any business he had with mushrooms, grass, sky would wait. He settled into the crotch of the tree, making himself a part of it, as stolid, as solid, as silent as a tree limb, and waited.

After a while, the dun-colored dog wandered off, followed by two grey brachets. The mastiff growled at each desertion but could not hold them past their hunger. Not wanting to challenge them over the boy, now gone beyond their sight and therefore beyond their reckoning, the mastiff growled to the rest of the pack and walked off, stiff-legged.

They followed.

Only when another five long, silent minutes were gone did the boy relax. He whistled then, through dry lips. It was not a sound of relief or a boy's long, piercing come-here whistle, but sounded instead like one of the small finches. He had been many months in the woods, and what speech he still had was interspersed with this kind of birdsong. When frightened, he grunted the warning call of the wild boar. The dogs had surprised but not frightened him. In the forest he was too quick for them and they could not climb trees.

This was his patch of woodland. He knew every bush and tangle of it, had marked it the way a wolf does, on the jumbled overground roots of the largest trees. Oaks were his favorites, having solid and low climbing limbs, though he did not call them *oak*. He had his own name for them, a short bark of sound.

By damming up one of the little streams, he caught fish when he needed them, bright silvery things with spotted backs, scarcely a hand's span long. He ate them raw. He did not eat other meat, but rather spied on little animals for entertainment—baby rabbits and baby squirrels when he could find their hidey-holes, and badgers in their setts. They made him laugh.

At night he called down owls.

Once he had scared a mother fox off her kill by growling fiercely and rushing her, but found he could not eat the remains. When he returned to the kill the next morning, the meat was gone; the scent of fox lay heavy on the ground.

The first time he had been set upon by the wild dogs, he'd been forced off his own meager dinner. They had scattered his small cache of mushrooms and berries, mouthing each piece, then spitting them out again. When he came down from the tree, he found what he could of his food, but it all smelled bad; he choked when he tried to eat it. He went hungry that night.

It was not the first time.

He was very thin, with knobs for knees and elbows like arrowpoints, and scratches all over his body, which was brown everywhere from the sun. His thatch of straight, dark hair fell across his face, often obscuring his eyes, which were as green as the woodland, with gold highlights, like rays of sun showing through.

He had never made a fire, was even a little afraid to, for he believed fire was a younger son of the lightning that he thought the very devil, for it felled several of the great trees and left only glowing embers. Still, if he worshipped anything, it was the trees that sheltered him, fed him, cradled him.

He laughed at the antics of baby animals but could not tell a joke.

He imitated birdsong but could not sing.

He liked the way rain ran down his hair and across his cheeks, but he did not cry. An animal does not cry.

He was eight years old and alone.

2. HISTORY

THE WHOLE TIME HE HAD LIVED ALONE IN THE woods came to one easy winter, one very wet spring, one mild summer, and one brilliant fall.

A year.

But for an eight-year-old that is a good portion of a lifetime. He remembered all of that year. What he could not recall clearly was how he had come to the woods, how he had come to be alone. What he could recall made him uneasy. He remembered it mostly at night. And in dreams.

He remembered a large, smoky hearth and the smell of meat drippings. A hand slapped his—he remembered this, though he could not remember who had slapped him or why. That was not one of the bad dreams, though. He could clearly recall the taste of the meat before the slap, and it was good.

He also remembered sitting atop a great beast, so broad his legs stuck out on either side, and no beast in the forest, not even the deer, was that broad. He could still remember three or four hands holding him up on the beast, steadying him. Each hand had a gold band on the next-to-last finger. And that was a good dream, too. He liked what he could recall of the animal's musty smell.

There was a third dream that was good. Some sweet, clean-smelling face near his own. And a name whispered in his ear. But that dream was the haziest of the good dreams. The word in his ear was softer than any birdcall. It was as quiet as a green inchworm on the spring bough. So quiet he couldn't make it out at all.

The other dreams were bad.

There was the dream of two dragons, one red and one white, asleep in hollow stones. They woke and screamed when he looked at them.

That dream ended horribly in flames. He could hear the screams, now dragon and now something else, as if everything screaming was being consumed by fire. The smell he associated with this dream was not so different from the smell of the small hare he had found charred under the roots of a lightning-struck tree.

And there was another dream that frightened him. A dream of lying within a circle of great stones that danced around him faster and faster, until they made a blurry grey wall that held him in. Awake, he avoided all rocky outcroppings, preferring the forest paths. At night he slept in trees, not caves. The hollow of an oak seemed safer to him than the great, dark, hollow mouths that opened into the hills.

The scariest dream of all was of a man and a sword. He knew it was a man and a sword, though he had no name for either of them. Sometimes the man pointed the sword at him, sometimes he held it away. The sword's blade was like a silvery river in which he could read many wonderful and fearful things: dragons, knights riding great beasts, ladies lying in barges on an expanse of water, and—most awful of all—a beautiful woman with long, dark hair that twisted and squirmed like snakes, who beckoned to him with a mouth that was black and tongueless.

He could not stop the dreams from coming to him, but he had learned how to force himself awake before he was caught forever in the dream. In the dream he would push his hands together, cross his forefingers, and say his name. Then his eyes would open—his real eyes, not his dream eyes—and he would slowly swim up out of the dream and see the leaves of the trees outlined in the light of the moon or against the flickering ancient pattern of stars. Only, of course, once he was awake he could not remember his name.

So he named himself: Star Boy. Moon Boy. Boy of the Falling Leaves. Whatever it was on that day or night that caught his fancy. Rabbit Boy. Badger Boy. Hawk-in-stoop Boy. Boy. He never said these names aloud.

He did not think of himself in the intimate voice; did not think *I* am or *I* want or *I* will. It was always Star Boy is hungry or Moon Boy wants to sleep or Boy of the Falling Leaves drinks or

Rabbit, Badger, Hawk-in-stoop Boy goes up the hill and over the dale. Only these were said in images, not words.

Time for him was always *now* except in dreams. His history, all of the past, made no more sense to him than the dreams. And as more and more of his human words fell away—having no one to use them with—so did his need for past or future. His only memory was in dreams.

3. HAWK

IT WAS THE TAG END OF FALL, AND THE SQUIR-
rels had been busy storing up acorn mast, hiding
things in holes, burying and unburying. The boy
had watched. He had even tried imitating them,
but could never recall where he had buried any
of the nuts, except for one handful, which when
unearthed tasted musky and smelled of dirt.

A double V of late geese, noisy and aggravated,
flew across the grey and lowering sky. He watched
them for a long time, yearning for something. He
did not know what. Shading his eyes with one
dirty hand, he followed their progress until the
last of them had disappeared behind a mountain.

"Hwonk," he cried after them. Then louder, "Hwahoooonk." He waited for a reply but none came. Unaccountably his right eye burned. He rubbed his fist in it and the fist was wet. Not a lot. But enough to make the dirt seem like filth.

Abruptly, he turned and ran down a deer track to the nearby river. He plunged in, paddling awkwardly near the edge, where the water pooled and slipped under exposed tree roots. He brought water up in cupped hands and splashed it on his face.

"Hwonk," he whispered to himself. Then he stood for a moment more. The cold water made his skin tingle pleasantly. When he climbed back up on the bank, the grass slippery underfoot, he shook himself all over like a dog and pushed the wet hair from his eyes.

He hummed as he walked, not a song, not even anything resembling a melody. It had no words, but a kind of comforting buzz. Then he yawned, his hand going up to his mouth as if it had a memory of its own. Finding a comfortable climbing tree, one he had used before, he got up in it, nestled in the place where two great limbs forked, and fell asleep. That it was day did not stop him from napping. He was alone. He made his own rules about time.

He had been asleep perhaps a quarter of an hour when a strange noise woke him; he did not move except to open his eyes. Caution had become a habit.

The sound that awakened him was not yippy like foxes or the long, howling fall of the dogs. It had teased into his dream and had changed the dream so abruptly that he awoke.

The call came closer.

Carefully he rose up a bit from the nest in the fork of the tree and crawled out along a thick branch that overlooked a clearing.

Suddenly something flapped over his head. He craned his neck and saw a hunting bird. She had a creamy breast and her tail had bands of alternating white and brown. Beak and talons flashed by him as she caught an updraft and landed near the top of a tall beech tree.

"Hwonk," he whispered, though he knew this was never such a bird.

No sooner had the falcon settled than the calling began again. It was an odd, unnatural, intrusive sound.

The boy looked down. On the edge of the wood stood a man, rather like the one in his dream, the one with the sword. He was large, with wide shoulders and red-brown hair that covered his face. There was a thin halo of hair around his head. When he walked across the meadow and then beneath the branch where the boy lay as still as leaves, the boy could see a round, pink area on the top of the man's head. It looked like a moon. A spotty, pink moon. The boy put his hand to his mouth so that he would not laugh out loud.

The man did not look up, did not notice the boy in the tree. His eyes were entirely on the tall beech tree and the magnificent bird near its crown. He swung a weighted string over his head and the string made an odd singing sound. The man whistled, and called, "Come, Lady. Come."

That was the sound that the boy had heard. The sound that had pulled him from his dream. Words.

The bird, though it watched the man carefully, did not move.

Neither did the boy.

4. CAPTURE

THE MAN AND THE BIRD EYED ONE ANOTHER FOR the rest of the short afternoon. In the tree, the boy watched them both. His patience with the scene below him was amazing, given that at one time or another his hands and his feet all fell asleep and he had an awful need to relieve himself.

Occasionally the bird would flutter her wings, as if testing them. Occasionally her head swiveled one way, then another. But she made no move to leave the beech.

The man seemed likewise content to stay. Except for making more circles around his head with the string, he remained almost motionless, though every now and again he made a clucking sound with his tongue. And he talked continuously to the bird, calling her names like "Hinny" and "Love," "Sweet Nell" and "Maid," in that same soft voice.

The boy took it all in, the bird in the tree, often still as a piece of stained glass, the sun lighting it from behind. And the man, with the thick leather glove on one hand, the whirring string in the other.

He wondered if the man would attempt, before night, to climb the tree after the bird, but he hoped that would not happen. The bird might then leave the tree; the tree, quite thin at the top, somewhat like the man, might break. The boy liked the look of the bird: her fierce, sharp independence, the way she stared at the man and then away. And the man's voice was comforting. It reminded the boy of something, something in his dreams. He could not remember what.

He hoped they would both stay. At least for a while.

When night came, they each slept where they were: the man right out in the clearing, his hands around his knees, the hawk high in her tree. The boy edged down from the tree, did his business, and was up the tree again so quietly none of the leaves slipped off into the autumn stillness.

He fell asleep once or twice that night but he did not dream.

In the morning the boy woke first, even before the bird, because he willed himself to. He watched as first the falcon shook herself into awareness, then the man below stretched and stood. If the boy had not seen them both sleeping, had only now wakened himself, he would have thought the two of them had not changed all the night.

The man was about to swing the lure above his head again when the falcon pumped her wings and took off from the tree at a small brown lark. The lark flew up and up, the hawk sticking closely behind, and soon they were on the very edge of sight.

The boy made slits of his eyes so he could watch, as first one bird and then the other took advantage of the currents of air. It almost seemed, he thought, as if the lark were sometimes chasing the hawk. He would have laughed aloud, but the man was too close beneath him.

The birds flew on, one above, one below, then circled suddenly and headed back toward the clearing, this time with the lark cleanly in the lead. The boy's hands in fists were hard against his chest as he watched, silently cheering first for the little bird, then for the following hawk.

Suddenly the lark swooped downward and the falcon hovered over it, a miracle of hesitation. Then with one long, perilous, vertical stoop, the hawk fell upon the lark, knocking it so hard the little bird tumbled over and over and over until it hit the ground not fifty feet from the man. Never looking away from her dying prey, the falcon followed it to earth. Then she sank her talons into the lark and looked about fiercely, as if daring anyone to take it from her.

The man walked quickly but without excess motion to the hawk. He nodded almost imperceptibly at her, speaking all the while in a continuous flow of soft words. Kneeling, he put one hand on her back and wings and with the other, the ungloved hand, hooded her so swiftly, the boy did not even see it till it was done. Then, standing, the man placed the bird on his gloved wrist, gathered up dead lark and lure with his free hand, and walked smoothly toward the part of the forest he had come from.

Only when the man had disappeared into the underbrush did the boy unwind himself from the tree. Man, falcon, and dead lark were all so fascinating, he could not help himself. He had to see more. So he ran to the edge of the woods and, after no more than a moment's hesitation, rather like the hawk before beginning her stoop, he plunged in after them.

5. TRAIL

THE MAN'S PATH THROUGH THE TANGLE OF UN-
derbrush was well marked by broken boughs and
the deep impression of his boot heels. He was
not difficult to follow. That should have made the
boy suspicious, but he was too caught up in the
hunt.

In his eagerness to track the man, the boy ne-
glected to note anything about the place, though
this was a caution he had learned well over his
year in the wild. Still, he knew he could always
track back along the same wide swath. So perhaps
his hunter's mind was working.

The thorny berry bushes scratched his legs,

leaving a thin red map from hip to ankle, but he was used to such small wounds. Once he trod on a nettle. But he had done so before. It would sting for a while, then slowly recede, leaving only a dull ache that would disappear when his attention was on something else.

Nothing—*nothing*—could dampen his excitement. Not even the tiny prickle of fear that coursed wetly down his back, between his shoulder blades. If anything, the fear sharpened his excitement.

He walked a few feet, stopped, listened, though it was a blowy day, clouds scudding across a leaden sky. Mostly what he heard was wind in trees. He relied, therefore, on his eyes, and followed the man's passage through fern and bracken, and the prints alongside a fast-running stream.

Several hours passed like minutes, and still the boy remained eagerly on the man's trail. Only twice did he actually glimpse the man again. Once he saw the broad back, covered with its leathern coat.

Coat. That was a word suddenly returned to him. Right after, he thought, *jerkin*. He didn't know why the two words came together in his mind. So dissimilar and yet—somehow—peculiarly the same. He stopped for a moment, giving the man plenty of time to move on, out of hearing, then whispered the two words aloud.

"Coat." The word was short, sharp, like a wild dog's bark.

"Jerkin." He liked that word better and said it over and over again several more times. "Jerkin. Jerkin. Jerkin." The last time he said it loud enough to become instantly wary. But when he looked around there was no sign of the man, and he relaxed. Going down into the stream, he bent over to get a drink, lapping at it like an animal. But when he lifted his head out of the water, he smiled and said the two words again. "Coat," he said. "Jerkin."

He found the man's easy trail again and ran a bit, to make up for the lost time.

The second time he saw the man, the man had turned on the path and looked right at him. The boy froze, willing himself to disappear into the brush the way a new fawn and badgers and even red foxes could. He closed his eyes so that they would not shine, so that the blinking of his eyes would not reveal where he was.

It must have worked, because when he peeked through slotted eyes at the man, the man looked right at him and did not seem to see him at all, but kept on stroking the falcon's shoulder and whispering something to the bird the boy could not hear. The man cocked his head to one side as if considering, as if listening, but the boy remained absolutely still. Then the man turned away and walked on.

The boy followed, but more carefully now, stopping frequently to hide behind a tree or a bush or kneel down in the bracken or lie in the furze. He did not actually have to see the man to know where he was. They were on a well-worn trail now, a path packed down by many years of use. The boy could read the faint boot marks as well as a sharp impression of deer feet, the softer scrapings of badger, even the scratchings of grouse. A dog pack had left its scat, and recently, too. That made the boy nervous, and he remarked the tallest trees in case he had to climb quickly.

His slow reading of this worn pathway occupied

him, and he was not paying attention to what lay ahead. So he was surprised when the road turned and opened onto a man-made clearing. A farmhouse squatted near the center of it.

The farmhouse explained the new scents he had been ignoring. For a moment, he hesitated by the last trees and stared.

"House," he whispered, afraid and yet not afraid. "House."

6. DREAM

THERE WAS A TRAIL OF SMOKE FROM THE HOUSE chimney and for a long time the boy watched it dreamily. He could almost smell a joint of meat roasting. He could almost remember the crackle of the skin.

Then as the man neared the house a chorus of dogs began to howl. The boy remembered the yellow mastiff and its pack all too well. He stepped into the shadow of the trees and ran back down the road.

As soon as he was too far away to hear the dogs, he forgot them, for his stomach was growling. He had had nothing to eat all day.

It was growing dark, and foraging had to be a

quick and careful matter. He found a walnut tree and gathered nuts, as well as late-growth bramble berries. Then, picking up a rock to help him crack the nuts open, he chose a sleeping tree and scrambled up it for the night.

The nuts and berries were enough to stop the fiercest of the hunger pangs. When he fell asleep, the moon hanging over him orange and full, he began to dream.

At first he dreamed of food. Food cooking on a large, open hearth. Then he dreamed of dogs scrabbling on the hearthstones for their share of the cooked meat. The dogs were enormous, with eyes as great as saucers, as great as dinner plates, as great as platters. They stared at him and through him and—in his dream—his skin sloughed off. He watched, skinless, as the dogs ate his skin. Then they turned and stared at him with their big eyes and growled.

He woke in a sweat, shivering, and threw the nutshells down from the tree. He touched his arm and his leg to assure himself that he was whole, skin and all. Then he promised himself he would not fall asleep again.

But he did.

This time he dreamed of women in black robes and black wings who fluttered around him. They opened their mouths, and bird sounds came out.

"Cause!" they screamed at him. "Cause!"

He held out his hand in the dream and was surprised how heavy it seemed. When he looked at it, it was encased in a leather glove with thumb and fingers stiff as tree limbs.

Only one of the black-robed women alighted on his hand, her nails sharp as talons, piercing right through the glove.

The pain woke him, and his one hand hurt as if something had pierced the palm. He licked the hurt place and there was a thin, salty, blood taste.

This time he did not fall asleep again but waited, shivering, for the dawn to finally come with its comforting rondel of birdsong.

7. HOUSE

HIS USUAL MORNING INCLUDED A DRINK OF water from the stream and a casual hunt for food. But this morning he saw, through the bare ligaments of trees, the thin line of chimney smoke.

House. The word came unbidden into his mind. And with the thought of house came the idea of food. Not berries and mushrooms and nuts and the occasional silver-finned, slippery fish torn open and devoured bones and all, but *food.* He was not sure what that meant anymore, but his mouth remembered, and filled with water at the thought.

So he crept back down the path to the edge of

the trees and squatted on his haunches, to stare avidly at the house.

There was a stillness about the house, except for that thread of smoke that seemed to unwind endlessly from the chimney.

At the prompting of his stomach, which ached as if it had suddenly discovered hunger for the first time, the boy left the sanctuary of the forest and ventured into the clearing. But he crept cautiously, like any wild thing.

There was a sudden flurry of sharp, excited cluckings. A familiar word burst into his head. *Hens!* He mouthed the word but did not say it aloud.

A high whinnying from one of the two outbuildings answered the hens. "Horse!" This time the boy spoke the word, his own voice reminding himself of the size of the beasts with their soft, broad backs that smelled of home.

He edged closer to the house, sniffing as he went, almost drinking in the odors, his chin raised and quivering.

Then the dogs began to bark and he turned sharply to run.

"Not so fast, youngling," said the man who loomed, suddenly, by his side and picked him off the ground by the shoulders. The man's voice was soft, not threatening, but the boy kicked and screamed a high, wild sound, and tried to slice at the man's face with his nails.

The man dropped him and grabbed both of the boy's hands with almost one motion, prisoning him as deftly as he had hooded the falcon.

The boy stopped screaming, stopped kicking, but he pulled away from the man, cowering, as if expecting a blow. His face was white, underneath the dirt, but his eyes were so dark as to be almost black, and hard and staring, the green-black of winterberries.

"Now hush ye, son," the man said in that soft, steady voice. "Hush, weanling, my young one, my wild one. Hush, you damned eelkin. I'll wash your face and hair and see what hides under that mop. Hush, my johnny, my jo." The soft murmuration continued as he marched the stone-faced boy all the way to the house and kicked open the door.

8. WILD THING

"MAG, FETCH ME A GREAT TOWEL. NELL, MY GIRL, put water in the tub. I've caught a wild thing that followed me home through the wood." The voice never got hard, though it got quite loud. "Quick now, the two of you. You know how it is with the wild ones."

Two women with kerchiefs binding their hair and long clay-colored gowns seemed to spring into being from the vast fireplace to do the man's bidding.

"Oh, sir," said the girl as she hauled the kettle full of water, "is it a bogle, all nekkid and brown like that? Is it a wodewose?" Her eyes grew big.

"It is a boy," said the man. "A sharp-eyed, underfed boy not much older than your own cousin Tom. And as for naked, well, he'd not been able to make clothes for himself after his own wore out, there in the middle of the New Forest, poor frightened thing. There are more than one of them put out in the woods nowadays. The nobles can send their extra sons off to a monastery as a gift of oblation, their hands wrapped in altar cloth and their inheritance clutched therein. But a poor man's son in these harsh times is oft left in the altar of the woods."

Mag appeared then with the toweling, shaking her head. "He looks not so much frightened, Master Robin, as fierce. Like one of your poor birds."

"Fierce indeed. And needing taming, I suspect, just like them. But first a bath, I think." The man smiled as he spoke, ever in that soft voice, while the two serving women clicked and clacked just like hens around the great tub. When at last they had emptied enough water in it and were satisfied with the temperature, Mag nodded and Master Robin dropped the boy in.

The boy had no fear of water, but it was not at all what he had expected. It was hot. *Hot!* River water, whatever the season, was always cold. Even in the lower pools—the ones he had dammed up for fishing—the water below the sun-warmed surface was cold enough to make his ankles ache if he stayed in too long.

He wanted to howl but he would not give his captors the satisfaction. He wanted to leap out of the bath, but the Robin-man's great hand was still on him. He didn't know what to do and indecision, in the end, made up his mind for him, for the fear and the warmth of the water together conspired to paralyze him. And the man kept speaking to him in that soft, steady, cozening voice.

The boy thought about the fawns in the forest, how they could disappear. How *he* had disappeared before when the man had stared at him. He closed his eyes to slits and willed himself to be gone, away from the man and his voice, away from the women and their hot water, away from the house.

But he had not slept well the last night, his dreams had prevented that. He was hungry, he was frightened, and he was—after all—only eight years old.

He closed his eyes and disappeared instead into a new dream.

In the new dream he was warm and safe and his stomach was full. He was cradled and rocked and sung sweet songs to by women in comforting black robes. They sang something he could remember just parts of:

> *Lullay, lullay, thou tiny child,*
> *Be sheltered from the wet and wild . . .*

But, he thought within the dream angrily, *I am wet and I am wild.* He made himself wake up by crossing his fingers, and found himself in a closed-in room.

Alone.

9. NAMES

UNTANGLING HIMSELF FROM THE COVERINGS, the boy crept to the floor and looked around cautiously. The room was low-ceilinged, heavily beamed. A grey stone hearth with a large fireplace was on the north wall. A pair of heavy iron tongs hung from an iron hook by the hearth. The fire that sat comfortably within the hearth had glowing red ember eyes that stared wickedly at him.

Suddenly something leaped from the red coals and landed, smoking, on the stones.

The boy jumped back onto the bed, amongst the tangle of covers, shaking.

The thing on the hearth exploded with a pop that split its smooth skin, like a newborn chick coming out of an egg. A sweet, tantalizing, familiar smell came from the thing. The boy watched as it grew cool, lost its live look. When nothing further happened, and even the red eyes of the fire seemed to sleep, he ran over, plucked up the hazelnut from the stones, and peeled it. His mouth remembered the hot, sweet, mealy taste even before he did.

He ran back to the bed and waited for something more to be flung out to him from the fire. Nothing more came.

But the nut had rekindled his hunger, and with it, his curiosity. He raised his head and sniffed. Besides the smell of roasted nut, beyond the heavy scent of the fire itself, was another, softer smell. The first part of it was like dry grass. He looked over the side of the bed and saw the rushes and verbena on the floor. That and the bed matting of heather supplied the grassy smell. But there was something more.

He scrambled across the wide bed and looked over the side. There, on a wooden tray, was food. Not mushrooms and berries, not nuts and silvery fish. But *food*. He bent over the food, as if guarding it, and looked around, his teeth bared.

He was alone.

He breathed in the smell of the warm loaf.

Bread, he thought. Then he spoke the name aloud.

"Bread!"

He remembered how he had loved it. Loved it covered with something. A pale slab next to the loaf had little smell.

Butter. That was it.

"But-ter." He said it aloud and loved the sound of it. "But-ter." He put his face close to the butter and stuck out his tongue, licking across the surface of the pale slab. Then he took the bread and ripped off a piece, dragged it across the butter, leaving a strange, deep gouge.

"Bread and but-ter," he said, and stuffed the whole thing in his mouth. The words were mangled, mashed in his full mouth, but he suddenly understood them with such a sharp insight that he was forced to shout them. The words—along with the pieces of buttered bread—spat from his mouth. He laughed and on his hands and knees picked up the pieces and stuffed them back in his mouth again.

Then he sat down, cross-legged by the tray, and

tore off more hunks of bread, smearing each piece with so much butter that soon his hands and elbows and even his bare stomach bore testimony to his greed.

At last he finished the bread and butter and licked the last crumbs from the tray and the floor around it.

There was a bowl of hot water the color of leaf mold on the tray as well. The bread had made him thirsty enough not to mind the color of the water and he bent over and lapped it up. He was surprised by the sweetness of the liquid and then knew—as suddenly as he had known the name of bread and butter—that it was not ordinary water. But he could not recall its name.

"Names," he whispered to himself, and named again all the things that had been given back to him, starting with the bread: "Bread. Butter. Horse. House. Hens. Jerkin. Coat." He liked the sound of these things and said the list of them again.

Then he added, but not aloud, *Master Robin, Mag, Nell.*

Patting his greasy stomach, he grunted happily.

He could not remember being this warm and this full for a long time. Maybe not ever.

Going back to the bed, he lay down on it, but he did not close his eyes. Instead he stared for a moment at the low-beamed ceiling where bunches of dried herbs hung on iron hooks. He had not noticed them before.

What else had he not noticed?

He sat up. There were two windows, and the light shining through them reminded him suddenly of the sun through the interlacing of the trees in the forest. This light fell to the floor in strange, dusty patterns. He crawled off the bed and over to the light, where he tried to catch the motes in his hand. Each time he snatched at the dusty beams, they disappeared, and when he opened his hand again, it was empty.

Standing, he looked out the window at the fields and at the forest beyond. There was a strong wind blowing. The trees were bending toward the east. He thrust his head forward, to smell the wind, and was surprised by the glass.

Hard air, he thought at first before his mind recalled the word *window*. He tried to push open the glass, but he could not move it, so he left that window and tried the other. He went back and forth between them, leaving little marks on the glass.

Angry then, he went to the wooden door in the wall next to the hearth and shoved his shoulder against it. It would not open.

So then he knew another name. *Cell*. He was in a cell. The fields he could see through the glass and the tall familiar trees beyond were lost to him. He put his head back and howled.

From the other side of the door came a loud, answering howl. One. Then another.

Dogs!

He ran back to the bed and hid under the covers and shivered with fear. There were no trees for him to climb. It was the first time in a long while that he had felt hopeless. That he had felt fear.

Wrapped in the covers, in the warmth, he fell asleep and did not dream.

10. THE BATED BOY

WHEN HE WOKE AGAIN THE ROOM WAS DARKER and the light through the windows shaded. There was a new loaf and a bowl of milk by the door.

The boy clutched the covers and listened, but he could hear no sound of dogs beyond the door. So he went over, warily, to the tray of food and cautiously looked at it sideways, through slotted eyes.

In a fit of sudden anger, an anger that smelled a good deal like fear, he kicked the bowl of milk over and screamed.

There was no answering scream beyond the door.

He went back to the bed, curled up in the

coverings as if he were in a nest, and willed himself back to sleep.

A few hours later he stood and urinated all around the bed, marking it for his own. Then, hungry, he went back to the door where the loaf waited on the tray. He ate it savagely, stuffing huge hunks into his mouth, and growling with each bite. When he was done, he sniffed around the place where the milk had spilled onto the floor, but it had all soaked in.

Bored and angry, he paced back and forth between the darkened windows and the door, faster and faster, until he broke into a trot. Finally he ran around the room, until he was dizzy and out of breath.

Then, standing in the very center of the room, he threw back his head to howl once again, but this time the howl died away into a series of short gasps and moans. He went back to the bed and curled into the covers and wept, something he had not done in a year.

When the sounds of his weeping had stopped and he drifted into a half sleep, the door into the room opened slowly. Master Robin entered and exchanged the empty tray for another, one with trenchers full of meat stew and milky porridge. Then he went over and stared down at the boy in the bed.

"Who are you, boy?" he whispered. "And how come you to our wood?" Then he knelt down and sat on the bed, stroking the boy's matted hair and brushing it from the wide forehead.

At last he murmured in that soothing, low voice, "It does not matter. First we'll tame you, then we'll name you." He smiled. "And then you'll claim your own."

The voice, the words, the warmth entered into the boy's dreams and, dreaming still, he smiled and wiped his finger along his cheek. Then the finger found its way into his mouth and he slept that way until dawn.

The next day was a repeat of the first, and the next and the next. There were trays of food, by the bed or by the door. The hearth fire seemed always to be glowing with embers. Occasional hazelnuts popped mysteriously out onto the hearth. Milk and stew appeared as if by magic. But the boy did not see anyone else, though his sharp ears picked up sounds from beyond the door. Mag's voice singing. Or Nell's. And—occasionally—the whine of a dog.

By the fifth day, the room smelled and the floors bore the filthy reminders of the boy's woods habits. But this time when he woke, Master Robin was in the room waiting for him to wake. He brought the tray of food to the bed and the boy sat up, involuntarily licking his upper lip.

When Master Robin sat on the bed, the boy reached over to grab the loaf.

The man slapped his hand.

The sting did not hurt so much as the surprise. And then there was a sudden memory of that other slap, when he had been holding the joint of meat, back . . . back . . . before the woods.

"Forgive . . ." the boy croaked, as if trying out a new tongue.

The man hugged him fiercely, suddenly. "Nothing to forgive, young one. Just slow down. The bread will not run away. It is the manners of the house and not the manners of the woods you must use here."

The words meant less than the hug, of course. The boy sat back warily, waiting.

Master Robin broke the bread into two sections. Then he picked up a wooden stick with a rounded end and stuck it in the bowl of porridge. "Spoon," he said. "Do you remember any such?" He was silent for a moment, then held out the thing to the boy. "Spoon."

The boy whispered back, "Spoon." He put out his hand, and his fingers, closing around the handle, remembered. He ate the porridge greedily, but with a measure of care as well, frequently stopping to check the man's reactions.

"Good boy. So you are no stranger to spoons. How long were you in the woods then, I wonder? Long enough to go wild. Ah well, we will tame you. I am not a falconer for nought. I know how to man a bird, how to tame it. I have a long patience with wild things. Eat then. Eat and rest. This afternoon, after we cut your hair and dress you, I'll take you to the mews to see the hawks."

11. ROOM

THE MAN LEFT WITH THE TRAY, AND THE BOY did not even try to follow him. There had been a promise. That much he understood. A promise of a trip outside. It was enough.

However, he was too awake and too excited to nap, and wandered instead around the room; not restlessly this time, or angrily. Instead he went slowly, cataloging the room's contents. It was *his* room now. He had made it his first by marking it and then by feeling safe in it. Now he needed to know every corner of it.

There was the bed in the center, with its rumpled covers. The heather stuffing smelled a bit of mould now. But it was a comforting smell and he was used to it. The rush-strewn floor was like-wise a bit off in its smell, like certain parts of the forest where there was too much bog and quaking earth. But the smell was familiar to him.

To one side of the bed was a small table that occasionally held a candle in an iron holder. He remembered its light when once he had awakened in the night. It had frightened him, then intrigued him. There was no candle now; instead a large bowl and jug stood there. He peered into them both. They were empty.

A great fire of logs burned on the hearth and to one side was a chair with a high back. It had arms carved with hawks' heads.

There was a tall wooden wardrobe standing by the side of the door. The handle for it was too high for him to reach. As if Master Robin's invi-tation had given him permission for exploration, he shoved the chair over to the wardrobe, scram-bled up on it, and poked and pushed at the latch until he had gotten it undone. Of course he could not then open the door of the wardrobe because the chair barred the way. It took him another moment to figure this out. When he pushed the chair out of the way, the door swung open on its own.

Inside he found a pile of fur robes of dark, soft hides that smelled like the fox who had snarled at him, like the wolves whose scent he had been careful to stay upwind of. He ran his hand over the robes, first the smooth way, then the other, and laughed. There was nothing to fear here.

He tugged one of the robes from the closet and wrapped it over his shoulders. Going down on all fours, he threw his head back and howled.

There was an answering howl from the other room.

Dogs! He dropped the fur robe and raced back to the bed where he cowered under the covers.

After a while, the dogs were quiet and the boy crept back off the bed. He went to the window and looked out. A cow grazed on the open meadow, fastened by a chain to its spot. Near it two brown dogs ran back and forth frantically. He had never seen them before. The cow did not seem disturbed by them, but the boy moved away from the window so that they might not see him. Perhaps, he thought, they were new to the pack.

When he sneaked back, the dogs were playing still, this time running to fetch something. He saw it was a stick, which they brought over and laid at the feet of the man. It made the boy wonder that they were so tame. Perhaps, then, they were not of the pack after all.

Daringly, the boy put his hand to the window but the dogs never noticed. Nor did the man. With his forefinger, the boy drew a line down the middle of the window several inches long. | He looked at it and then, ever so carefully, drew a line across the middle. ✝ After a moment's thought he drew a round thing on the top. ✝ Then he stopped and shook his head. The figure was incomplete. It needed something. He stood back from the window trying to puzzle it out, but the lines blurred together, faded.

When he turned around, Master Robin was standing in the room. Next to him were the two women. All three of them were smiling.

12. MEWS

THE OLDER WOMAN, MAG, STOPPED SMILING AS she crossed the threshold, wrinkling her nose as she glanced around the room.

The girl cried out, "Master Robin! The smell!"

"Hush ye!" the man said. He meant it sharply but his voice was not sharp.

The boy stood stone still as they approached him.

"Now, boy, now, little one . . ." the man's low, cozening voice began. He reached for the boy and, for a moment, that was all. Then his large hand gripped the boy's.

The boy trembled in the man's grasp. But when

the two women drew nearer and the girl put her hand on his arm, the boy snarled, a deep, chesty sound, and bared his teeth.

She drew back at once.

"You are a boy, not a beast," the man said gently. "You are a child of God, not . . ."

The boy's eyes rolled up in his head.

"Are you going to faint on me, boy?" the man asked.

But the boy was staring at the rooftree. "God," he whispered.

Mag and Nell crossed themselves quickly. The boy did the same, with his free arm.

"Nor Satan's imp then," Nell said.

"Of course not, you silly wench." For the first time there was exasperation in the man's voice. "Just a child. Gone feral. How often need I tell you so?"

Mag clucked like a hen and smoothed down her apron. "I am not so daft, Master Robin. Tell me what to do."

"The trews, woman. Bring them me."

She handed him the grey trousers with the drawstring waist. He prisoned the boy's two hands with his one big one, but not so as to hurt him, then with the other—and Mag's help—drew the pants on the boy one leg at a time.

At first the boy shook all over and whimpered. But he did not fight. He was too curious and, though he could not have explained why, found it vaguely familiar as well.

The shirt, when it went over his head, was more familiar still. He smoothed it down his chest, liking the feel of the cloth against him. In his memory there was another such shirt, one that came down to his knees, of a softer weave. It had kept him warm, he remembered, until it had—at last—fallen apart sometime in late spring. Only he did not remember spring. He thought of it as the warm time, when the river ran swiftly over the stones.

Then the man put a strange harness over the boy's head and around each shoulder and across his chest and back. It was plaited of rope and had a lead that Master Robin tied around his own wrist.

That reminded the boy of the cow tied out in the field, but he did not try to pull away. It made him feel as if he were part of the man and he liked that.

Master Robin sent the two women scuttling out of the room with a single word. "Go!" he said. They ran out like badgers scattering back to the sett. The boy laughed as they closed the door behind them. Master Robin laughed, too.

"So," the man said, "you can laugh and you can cry and you can speak some. You are no idiot left out by a father, no simpleton cast out of his town. I wonder why you were set adrift?" He stroked his beard as he spoke in that low voice.

The boy did not understand the question. What was *adrift?* What was *simpleton?* What was *town?*

"Would you like to see the birds in the mews?"

That at least he understood. *Birds.* He nodded.

"Well. And well." Master Robin pulled the boy close to him by the lead, then patted him on the head. "Tomorrow we will worry about your hair."

The birds were housed in a long, low building, with small windows of thinned-down horn.

"The mews," Master Robin said as they entered. He gave name to other things as they walked through the room. "Door. Perch. Bird. Lamp. Rafters."

Mimicking his tone, the boy repeated each word with a kind of greed, as if he could not get enough of the names. As he spoke, his face took on the same look it had when he had smelled the first loaf of bread, eyes squinting, head up, in feral anticipation.

They walked slowly, kicking up sawdust as they went. The boy took in everything as if it were both his first and his hundredth time in such a place.

He stood at last in front of a trio of hooded birds on individual stands where the heavy sacking screens hanging from the perches moved in the slight wind like castle banners. It looked as if he were about to speak. Instead he leaned forward, trembling, straining against the harness and lead.

Just then the two brown dogs, mixed-breed hounds, bounded into the mews.

The boy screamed and tried to run.

"Stay, damn you, stay!" the man shouted, whether to the dogs, the boy, or the hawks now agitated on their perches, their feathers ruffling —it was not clear.

The boy continued to shriek, his eyes wild.

The man turned to the dogs. "Sit!" he thundered, holding up his hand.

The two dogs immediately sat, tongues lolling. The smaller dog moved forward on its hind end, closer to the man, whining.

"Lie down," he thundered at them.

They lay down. The boy stopped shrieking but hid, trembling, behind the man. The hawks still fluttered, but at last even they quieted.

The man dragged the boy around in front of him by the rope. "These dogs will not harm you if I tell them so. They will guard you. They will be your friends."

The boy's trembling did not cease, but he was silent.

Holding the boy close, the man brought him to the dogs. "He is our boy," the man said. "You will *guard*. Now, *greet*." The larger of the two dogs crawled on its belly to the boy and licked his foot. The smaller dog followed. "Now, boy, pat their heads. Pull their ears. Let them hear thy voice."

He showed the boy what to do, but the boy was still too frightened, until the smaller dog suddenly rolled over on its back and showed the boy its belly. He touched its belly tentatively and then threw his head back and laughed. The dog flipped over and lay its quivering head on his bare foot. Bending down, the boy patted the dog's head. Then he pulled its ears.

"Dog," he said, in a voice that consciously mimicked the man's deep tones.

But he did not dare touch the larger dog. He just nodded at it.

"Enough for one lesson," the man said. "Time to eat." And they walked through the long, low building and into the slanting light of the fall day, which was a surprise to them both.

"Dog," the boy said as they walked past the corner of the building, where waist-high nettles hid the broken stones of an old wall. The small dog came to him, and trotted contentedly at his heels all the way into the house.

13. DOG

THE SMALL DOG SLEPT AT THE BOY'S BEDFOOT until the middle of the night, when it got up and crept into the bed with him. The new heather in the mattress reminded the boy of the outdoors and the warmth of the dog recalled a time well before memory. He stirred slightly and slipped into a dream that was softer and gentler than any dreaming he had had in a year.

But after a while, the dog began to dream, too, of coursing after hare through the bracken. His legs scrabbled on the bedclothes and he scratched the boy's leg, not drawing blood, but pulling him swiftly out of sleep.

The boy woke disoriented and then, remembering, stuck his face in the dog's side, drinking deeply of the smell.

"Dog," he said, then raised his head and looked about.

The room was partly lit by light streaming in through the window. The boy rose from the bed, careful so as not to disturb the sleeping dog, and padded over to the lighted sill.

Under a full harvest moon, round and orange, shadows shifted across the field as if dream waves rolled across a dream ocean. The boy could just see the corner of the mews. And seeing the mews, he remembered the trio of birds on their perches shaking their wings in fear.

Something about those birds was important to him, but he did not know what. He only knew, suddenly and with fierce conviction, that he had to go to them.

He had gone to bed wearing the shirt Master Robin had put on him. It hung almost to his knees. He could not, himself, get into the trews. He did take the harness, though, thinking it part of his outfit, and carefully threaded his arms through it, wrapping the leadline around his arm three times to keep it out of his way. He began to tiptoe toward the door.

The dog roused at once, wagging its not inconsiderable tail.

"Dog," the boy whispered. The animal left the bed and came right over to him. "Sit!" But the boy's voice had none of the authority of the man's, and the dog remained standing at his side, its tail banging against his legs at every other beat.

The door was not open but it was not locked. The boy found this out when he pushed against it. It creaked only slightly. When he went out into the big hall, trailed by the dog, there was no one there but the mother dog drowsing on the hearthstones. Only coals remained of the roaring fire.

The boy was entirely silent as he moved across the floor, but the little dog's toenails clacketed on the stones. It was a comforting sound, though, and the boy smiled at it. The sound disturbed the older dog's sleep, however, and she looked up for a moment, lazily puzzled, before settling back with a contented sigh.

After several minutes the boy found the outside door. He had excellent night sight from his year in the forest, and besides, he could smell the outdoors through the space where door and wall did not exactly fit. It was a matter of moments till he could figure out the lifting of the latch, having watched the man do it.

He pulled the door open.

The little dog raced out before him, sniffing eagerly at the night air, then running to the nettles at the corner of the mews where it smelled the markings of its mother.

For a moment the boy stopped to look at the black-and-white shadow waves. There was a slight breeze blowing past the mews and over the field to the forest beyond. He could smell the musty mews, the birds, possibly the cow and horse in the stone barn beyond. Drawing himself up, recited the litany he had learned that afternoon: "Door," he said. "Perch. Bird. Lamp. Rafters." Then he walked to the mews door.

His hand was barely on the latch when a dog leaped upon him. Instinctively his hand went to guard his throat and the dog's teeth found only his wrist. In the moon's light he saw it was the dun dog and realized his mistake. The wind had been blowing *to* the woods. Not *from* it. He'd had no warning of the pack.

He screamed, a high piercing scream. The dun suddenly slackened its grip as the little brown dog, who'd slept so loyally on the boy's bed, leaped onto its back, savaging it with sharp teeth.

Then the pack was on them, the pair of grey brachets, the three small terriers harrying at the boy's heels. The yellow mastiff stood to one side, watching its packmates, waiting to move in at the kill.

And then just as suddenly the pack was scattered by a fierce, dark shadow. The loud, howling mother dog, having left the fire at the boy's first scream, waded into them. She found the terriers, grabbing one with her teeth and, shaking it three times fiercely, breaking its neck. The other two ran yipping across the meadow, disappearing entirely into the shadows of the corn.

The brachets wrenched about to face her and the dun threw the little dog off its back, and faced her as well. That could have been the end of her fight. There were still three against her. To save herself she needed to turn and run. But then, from behind her came a low, throaty growl. The yellow mastiff moved, stiff-legged, toward her, cutting off any retreat.

The boy began to tremble, but when the little dog hobbled to his side, favoring one front leg, and growled back at the mastiff, the boy's trembling became anger instead of fear. He unwrapped the leadline from his arm and in one savage movement flung himself on top of the dun dog, throttling its neck with the rope as hard as he could. He wasn't strong enough to kill it, but he managed to cut off its breathing and it dropped beneath him.

As if that were some kind of signal, the rest of the pack—the brachets and the mastiff—fell upon the mother dog. She screamed once, but the sound was drowned out by a sudden loud cracking of a horse whip.

"GET . . . AWAY . . . YOU . . . " came Master Robin's voice, and the whip snapped again, opening up the back of one of the brachets. And then again, the left front leg of the other.

The mastiff smelled the blood and would have stayed on, but the man banged its nose with the heavy leather butt end of the whip and it sprang away from the fight. Still growling, it backed up in its stiff-legged way till it felt the first of the corn at its back. Then it turned and melted away into the shadows. The brachets followed, howling. The dun, gasping, rose and stumbled after them.

Still trembling, the boy started toward the corn-field, but was caught up short by the man holding the trailing end of the leadline.

"Let them go," the man said, his voice soft again. "They will do us no harm now, my boy."

Suddenly the boy found himself sobbing. "Dog," he said. "Dog." He dropped to his knees and smoth-ered the little dog with hugs.

Master Robin picked the boy up in one arm, the little dog in the other. "Our dogs will be well again," he said. "Let us tend them, shall we?"

"Yes," the boy said. "Yes." He buried his head against the man's broad shoulder for a moment, then looked past him. The mother dog, limping, bleeding slightly from a bite up high on her neck, was right behind. When he saw this, the boy re-laxed and nuzzled against the man as a young pup will do with its own.

14. NAME

IT TOOK THEM THE REST OF THE NIGHT, MAN
and boy working together, to bind up the dogs'
wounds. The wounds were not deep, but there
were many and they bled profusely. The mother
dog lay patiently by the now-roaring fire while the
man put poultices on the open sores and sewed
up the raw edges of the bites with coarse black
thread. But the smaller dog would not be still except with its head on the boy's lap.

By first light they were done, but with Mag and
Nell stirring about, neither boy nor man wanted
to try and sleep.

"The mews then?" the man asked at last.

"*Master Robin*—and after what happened?" Mag protested, waving her hands about.

The boy gave her a pitying look.

"The birds still must be tended," the man said. "And I will take the whip. But I doubt that pack will be back. There's easier pickings in the woods."

They went out, man and boy, together.

Except for patches of blood-sodden earth and the dead terrier by the mews door, there was no sign of the war that had been fought. They buried the terrier—so small and pathetic in the morning light. The boy did not wonder at it. He had seen his fill of dead things in the wood.

The mews was cool and shadowy; it smelled of must and age. The boy went eagerly in after the man, and in a quiet voice recited his lesson.

"Door. Perch. Bird. Lamp. Rafters."

The man turned to look at him and nodded, careful not to laugh. They stared at one another for a long moment, then tracked through the sawdust on the floor side by side.

When at last they were before the trio of birds, Master Robin stood, hands behind his back, nodding. The boy echoed his stance.

"Bird," the boy said, his voice husky.

"Mine," the man said as if in answer. He took care to speak as solemnly as the boy. "Mine because they have given some part of themselves to me. But not all. And not forever." He let the boy take that in before continuing. "I would not want them to give me all. And every day I must earn their trust again."

"Again," the boy said, nodding.

"With wild things," the man said, turning his head slightly to watch the boy, his eyes narrowing, "there is no such word as *forever*."

The boy listened intently.

"I stood three nights running with the goshawk there," said the man, nodding toward the bird furthest to the left. "He was on my fist the whole time."

"Tied?" the boy asked. It was a new word and an old one for him.

"Aye."

The boy seemed to consider this, as if he knew it had been a wise thing to do. "Tied."

"When he bated, I put him back on my fist again. And again. And again. I sang to him. I spoke words to him."

"My hinny, my jo," the boy said in a passable imitation of the man's voice. The man was momentarily stunned. "My hinny, my jo," the boy repeated.

"Aye. And stroked his talons with a feather and gave him meat. And, after three days without sleep, he allowed himself to nap on my fist. He *gave* himself to me in his sleep."

"In his sleep," the boy said, wondering if the hawk could dream.

"The peregrine there," Master Robin said, indicating the middle bird. "Now she is my oldest bird. A beauty. An *eyas*. Like all females, she is strong and calm."

"Eyas. Oldest." The words were equally strange to the boy.

The third bird suddenly stirred.

"That means I took her from the nest myself. Nearly lost an eye doing it, but . . ." The man stopped, aware the boy was no longer listening. Instead he was straining to watch the third bird, staring up at it.

"Ah, that one. He's a *passager,* wild caught but not yet mature."

The hawk stirred again, as if it knew it was

being talked about. The bell on its jess rang out.

At the sound, the boy jumped back.

"You like my merlin best, then?" the man asked in his low voice.

The boy turned sharply, stared at the man wide-eyed. His mouth dropped open and he put his hands out as if he had suddenly been turned blind.

Master Robin gathered the boy in his arms. "What is it, then? What is it, my boy, my passager, my wild one? What did I say? What have I done?"

The boy tore from his arms, and turned again to the bird who, unaccountably, began to rock back and forth from one foot to another, its bell jangling madly.

As if he, too, were a bird on a perch, the boy began to rock back and forth. "Name," he cried out. "Name."

The man stared at the boy and bird and finally, with a shock of understanding, he plunged his hand into the nearby water barrel. Then he reached for the boy. With his finger he drew a cross on the boy's forehead, one swift line down, a second across, under the tangle of elfknots in his hair.

"I baptize thee Merlin, my child. Somehow your name is the bird's. In the name of the Father and of the Son and of the Holy Spirit. Amen."

"Amen," the boy said, and smiled up at the man. "I . . . am . . . Merlin." And memory as well as language came flooding through him as he was given back his own true name.

Light.

Morn.

"Mother, I think often of my lost one, my hawk-let, my Merlin."

"Do not say his name here, my daughter. Do not summon up the past."

"But, Mother, he is not just past, but future as well. As are all children."

"You must think upon the Lord God, my daughter."

"Will He think upon my child?"

"God watches over all wild things, my daughter, for they neither worry about nor pity their own condition. Perhaps your son is the greater for this exile in the woods."

"Perhaps, Mother, he is dead."

"Then he is with God the sooner. And we are still here, laboring away at our daily rounds. To your prayers now. Think no more of what has been, but what shall be."

The bells ring for matins, like the sound of a tamed hawk's jesses, like the voices of angels making the long and perilous passage between heaven and earth.

AUTHOR'S NOTE

The story of Merlin, King Arthur's great court wizard, is not one story but many, told by different tellers over nearly fifteen centuries. In some of the tales he is a Druid priest. In others, a seer. In still others he is a shape-shifter, a dream-reader, a wild man in the woods.

And in some of the old tales, Merlin is a child born of a princess in a nunnery, his father a demon.

I have taken some of the bits and pieces of those old stories and woven them into a story that incorporates some history and some hawking. In the Middle Ages, because of wars or famine or plague, many children were actually abandoned in the woods. There they were left to—in the Latin ecclesiastical phrase—*aliena misericordia*—the kindness of strangers. Historically, until the eighteenth century, the rate of known abandonments in some parts of Europe was as high as one in four children, an astonishing and appalling figure.

Hawking, or falconry, is the art of using falcons, hawks—even eagles and owls—in hunting game. It is a very ancient pastime, practiced by humans even before they learned to write. Falconers have their own special words: a male hawk (which is smaller than the female) is called a *tercel*. The larger female hawk is called a *falcon*. An *eyas* is a hawk taken from the nest when fully fledged but as yet unable to fly. But the wild-caught immature bird is a *passager*.

A *merlin* is a small falcon, sometimes called a pigeon hawk in America. It was once much used in English falconry.

—J. Y.